PIRATES

© Aladdin Books Ltd 2010

Designed and produced by
Aladdin Books Ltd

**First published in 2010
in the United States**
by Stargazer Books,
distributed by
Black Rabbit Books
P.O. Box 3263
Mankato, MN 56002

Illustrators
Susanna Addario, Simone Boni, Lorenzo Cecchi,
Fiametta Dogi, Francesca D'Ottavi, L.R. Galante,
Lorenzo Pieri, Roberto Simone – McRae Books,
Florence, Italy.

Library of Congress Cataloging-in-Publication Data

Pipe, Jim, 1966-
    Pirates / Jim Pipe.
        p. cm. -- (True stories and legends)
    Includes index.
    ISBN 978-1-59604-198-1
    1. Pirates--Juvenile literature. I. Title.
    G535.P485 2009
    910.4'5--dc22

                                                2008016500

TRUE STORIES AND LEGENDS

PIRATES

Jim Pipe

Stargazer Books
Mankato, Minnesota

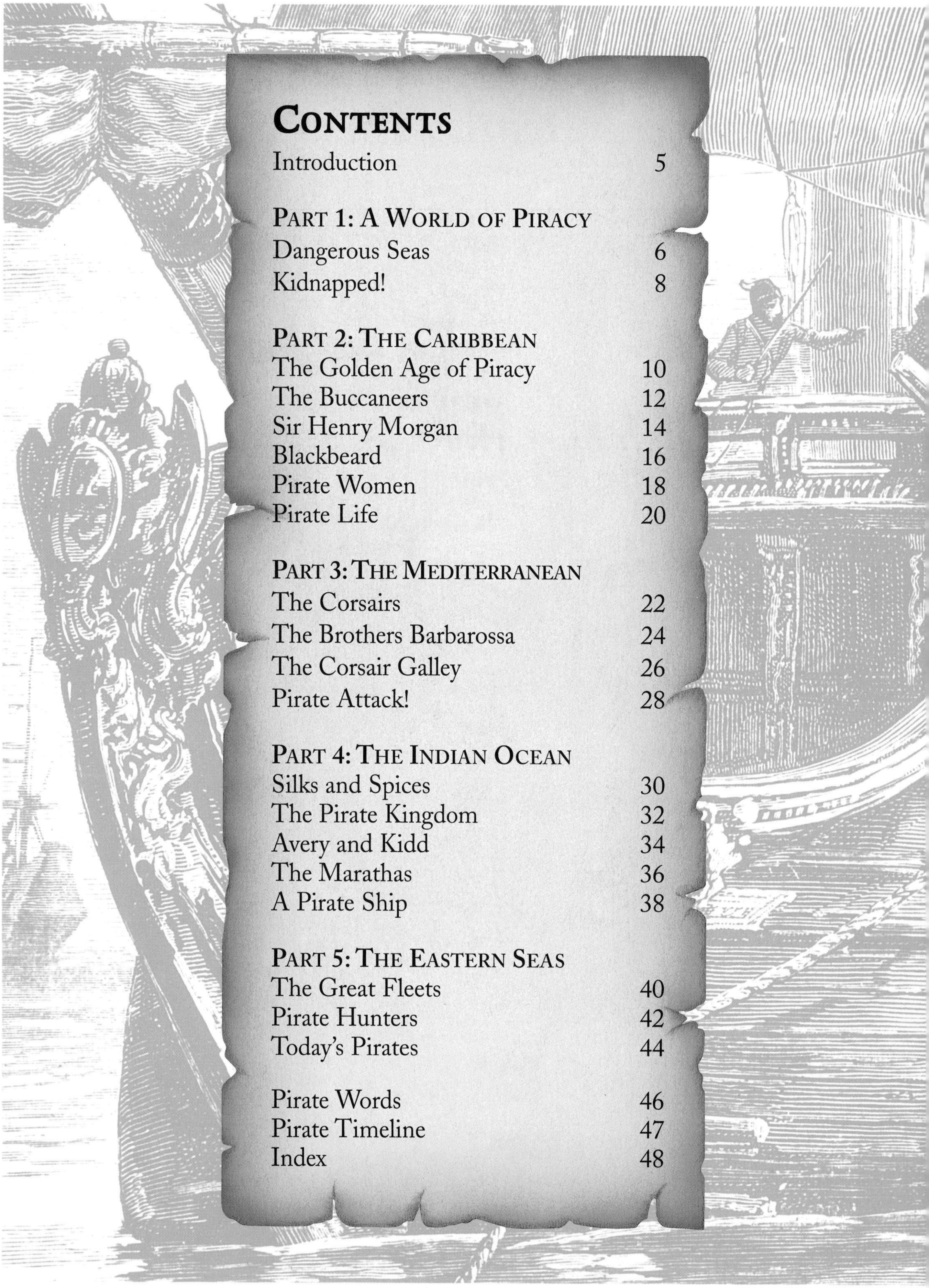

CONTENTS

Introduction 5

PART 1: A WORLD OF PIRACY
Dangerous Seas 6
Kidnapped! 8

PART 2: THE CARIBBEAN
The Golden Age of Piracy 10
The Buccaneers 12
Sir Henry Morgan 14
Blackbeard 16
Pirate Women 18
Pirate Life 20

PART 3: THE MEDITERRANEAN
The Corsairs 22
The Brothers Barbarossa 24
The Corsair Galley 26
Pirate Attack! 28

PART 4: THE INDIAN OCEAN
Silks and Spices 30
The Pirate Kingdom 32
Avery and Kidd 34
The Marathas 36
A Pirate Ship 38

PART 5: THE EASTERN SEAS
The Great Fleets 40
Pirate Hunters 42
Today's Pirates 44

Pirate Words 46
Pirate Timeline 47
Index 48

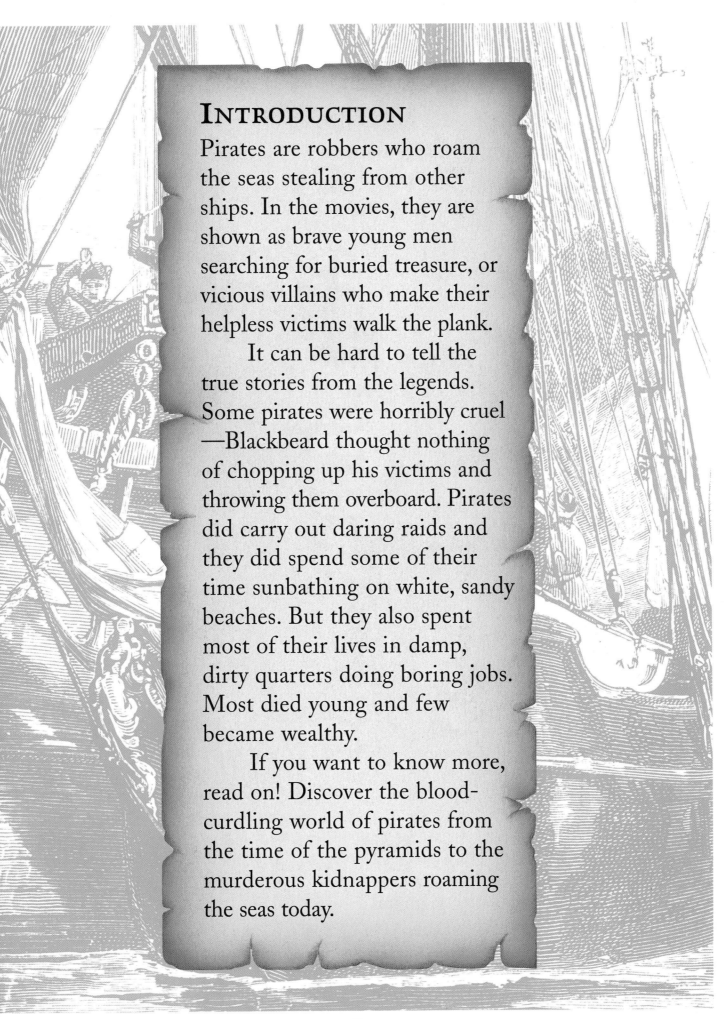

INTRODUCTION

Pirates are robbers who roam the seas stealing from other ships. In the movies, they are shown as brave young men searching for buried treasure, or vicious villains who make their helpless victims walk the plank.

It can be hard to tell the true stories from the legends. Some pirates were horribly cruel —Blackbeard thought nothing of chopping up his victims and throwing them overboard. Pirates did carry out daring raids and they did spend some of their time sunbathing on white, sandy beaches. But they also spent most of their lives in damp, dirty quarters doing boring jobs. Most died young and few became wealthy.

If you want to know more, read on! Discover the blood-curdling world of pirates from the time of the pyramids to the murderous kidnappers roaming the seas today.

PART 1: A WORLD OF PIRACY —DANGEROUS SEAS

On a cruise today, you don't expect to watch out for pirates. Around 300 years ago, however, hundreds of pirates roved the seas, cutting throats and sinking ships from the Caribbean to the China Seas.

As well as Spanish gold, pirates stole anything that could be sold, from spices and sugar to wine and slaves. Few ships were safe from attack, especially in seas where there was no navy to hunt pirates down.

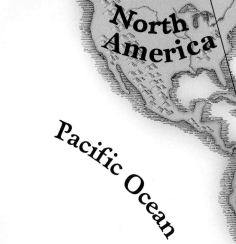

Caribbean Here, Spanish treasure ships attracted pirates known as "buccaneers."

North America

Atlantic Ocean

Pacific Ocean

South America

▲ **Hooks and Peglegs**
Storybook pirate Captain Hook has a hook for a hand, while Long John Silver has an eye patch and a wooden leg. Real pirates also lost limbs or had their faces smashed by cannon balls. Yet the pirates played by 1930s movie star Errol Flynn hardly got a scratch! ▶

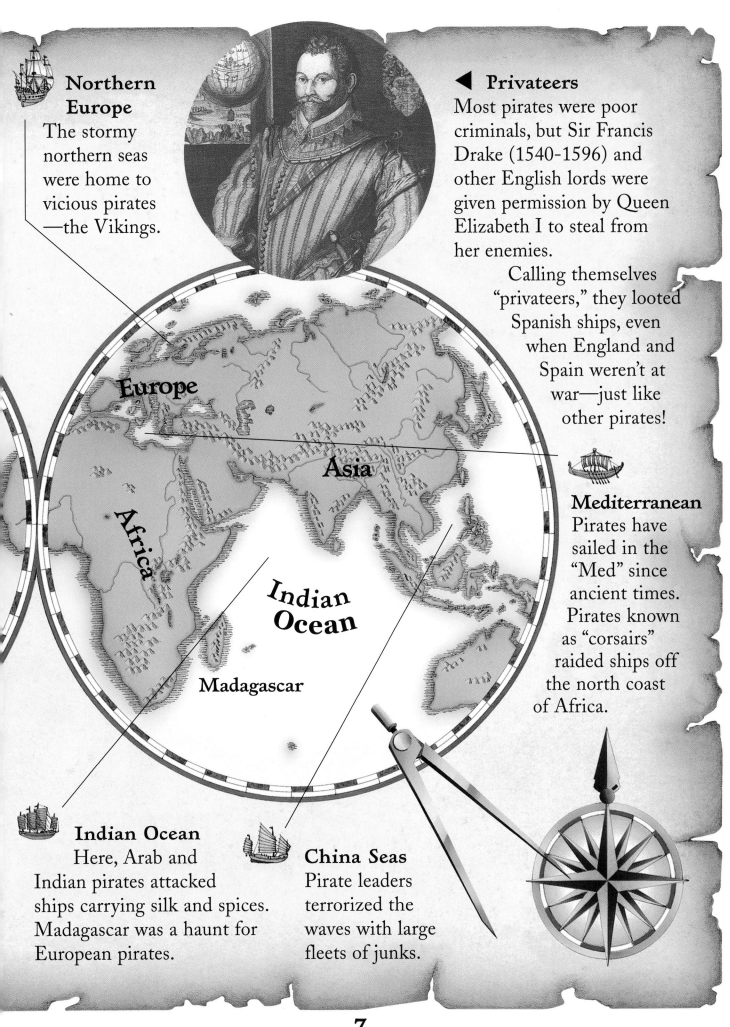

Northern Europe

The stormy northern seas were home to vicious pirates —the Vikings.

◀ Privateers

Most pirates were poor criminals, but Sir Francis Drake (1540-1596) and other English lords were given permission by Queen Elizabeth I to steal from her enemies.

Calling themselves "privateers," they looted Spanish ships, even when England and Spain weren't at war—just like other pirates!

Mediterranean

Pirates have sailed in the "Med" since ancient times. Pirates known as "corsairs" raided ships off the north coast of Africa.

Europe

Asia

Africa

Indian Ocean

Madagascar

Indian Ocean

Here, Arab and Indian pirates attacked ships carrying silk and spices. Madagascar was a haunt for European pirates.

China Seas

Pirate leaders terrorized the waves with large fleets of junks.

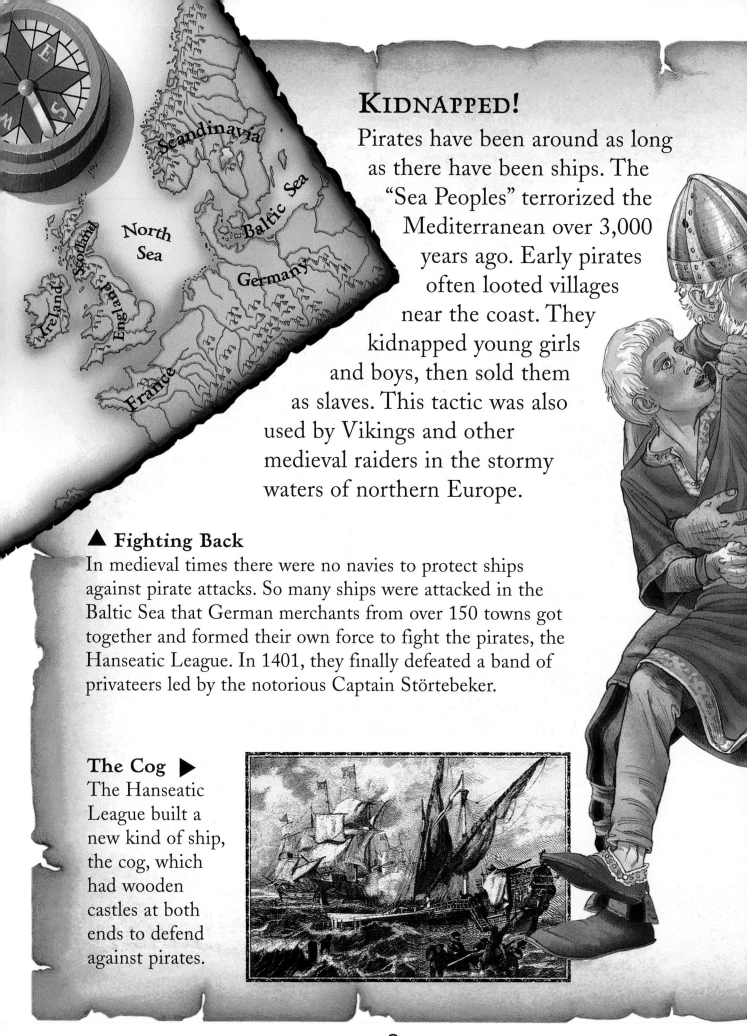

KIDNAPPED!

Pirates have been around as long as there have been ships. The "Sea Peoples" terrorized the Mediterranean over 3,000 years ago. Early pirates often looted villages near the coast. They kidnapped young girls and boys, then sold them as slaves. This tactic was also used by Vikings and other medieval raiders in the stormy waters of northern Europe.

▲ Fighting Back

In medieval times there were no navies to protect ships against pirate attacks. So many ships were attacked in the Baltic Sea that German merchants from over 150 towns got together and formed their own force to fight the pirates, the Hanseatic League. In 1401, they finally defeated a band of privateers led by the notorious Captain Störtebeker.

The Cog ▶

The Hanseatic League built a new kind of ship, the cog, which had wooden castles at both ends to defend against pirates.

8

Longship ▶
Viking ships had a shallow hull for river raids.

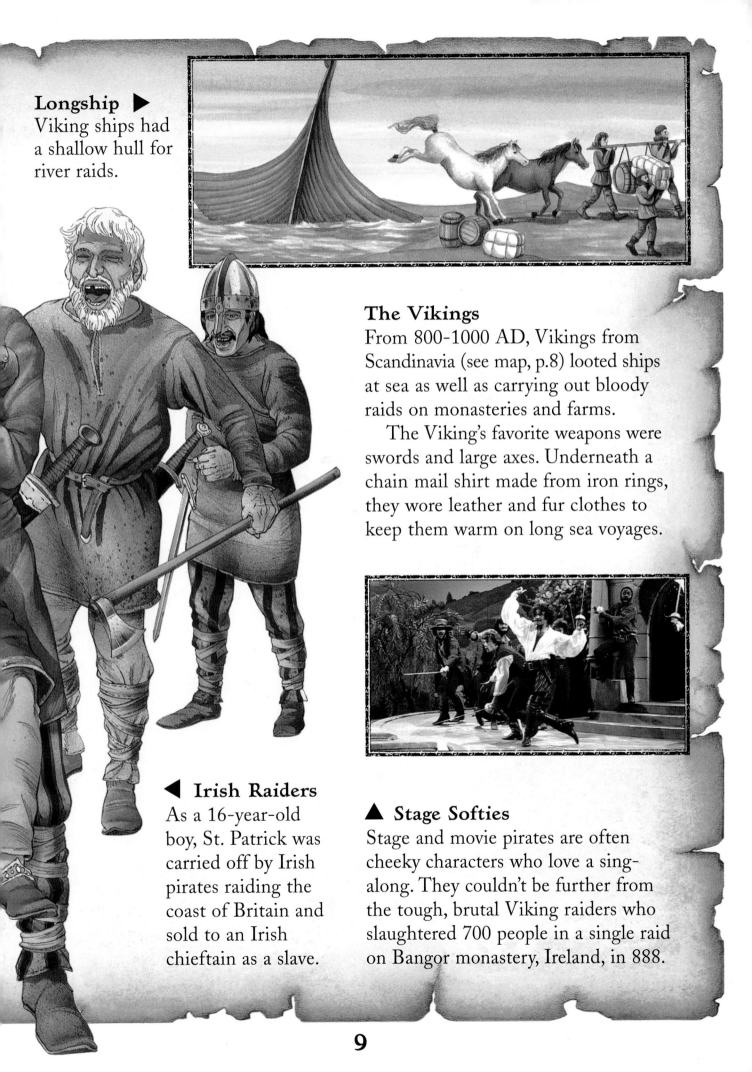

The Vikings

From 800-1000 AD, Vikings from Scandinavia (see map, p.8) looted ships at sea as well as carrying out bloody raids on monasteries and farms.

The Viking's favorite weapons were swords and large axes. Underneath a chain mail shirt made from iron rings, they wore leather and fur clothes to keep them warm on long sea voyages.

◀ **Irish Raiders**
As a 16-year-old boy, St. Patrick was carried off by Irish pirates raiding the coast of Britain and sold to an Irish chieftain as a slave.

▲ **Stage Softies**
Stage and movie pirates are often cheeky characters who love a sing-along. They couldn't be further from the tough, brutal Viking raiders who slaughtered 700 people in a single raid on Bangor monastery, Ireland, in 888.

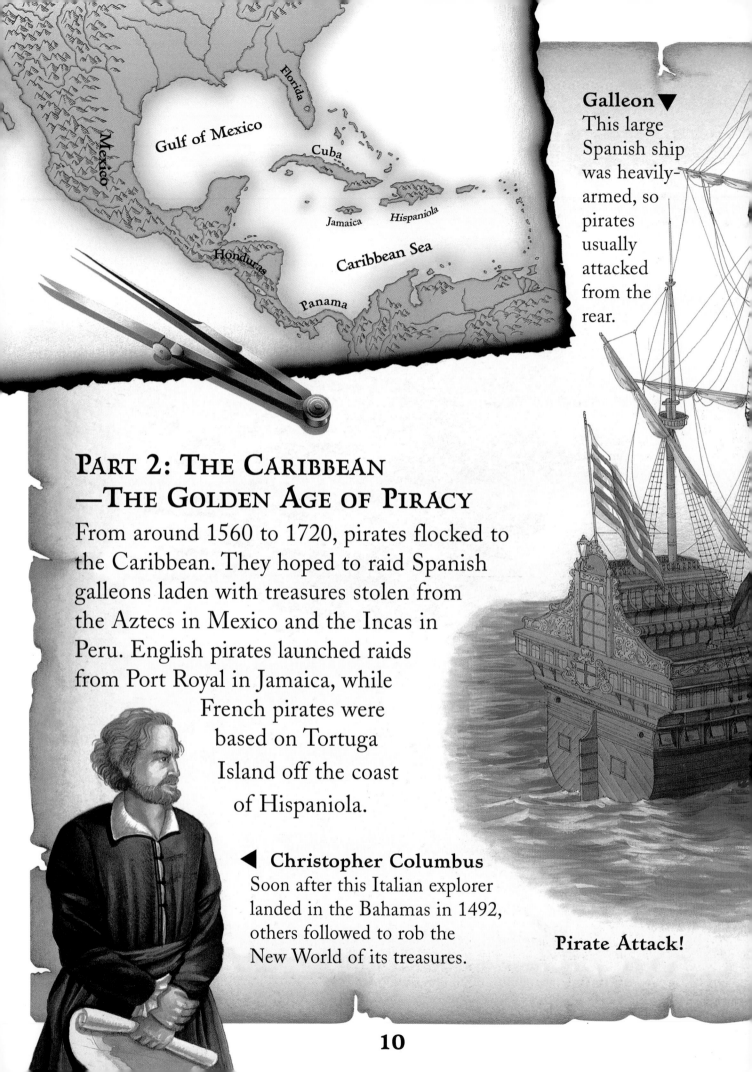

Mexico

Gulf of Mexico

Florida

Cuba

Jamaica   Hispaniola

Honduras

Caribbean Sea

Panama

Galleon ▼
This large Spanish ship was heavily-armed, so pirates usually attacked from the rear.

PART 2: THE CARIBBEAN —THE GOLDEN AGE OF PIRACY

From around 1560 to 1720, pirates flocked to the Caribbean. They hoped to raid Spanish galleons laden with treasures stolen from the Aztecs in Mexico and the Incas in Peru. English pirates launched raids from Port Royal in Jamaica, while French pirates were based on Tortuga Island off the coast of Hispaniola.

◀ Christopher Columbus
Soon after this Italian explorer landed in the Bahamas in 1492, others followed to rob the New World of its treasures.

Pirate Attack!

▼ Pirate Brigantine

Though small, pirate ships were fast and easy to handle. Some were given scary names like "The Black Angel."

Paying His Way ▶

This 18th-century scientist, William Dampier, became a pirate to pay for his trips around the world. He used the notes he kept of his voyages to write a bestselling book.

▲ The Conquistadors

During the 16th century, small bands of Spanish soldiers, the "Conquistadors," quickly conquered the huge Aztec and Inca empires in Mexico and Peru. The local peoples' stone weapons were no match for the swords and cannons of the Spanish. Millions were wiped out by diseases brought by the Europeans.

Knife and scabbard

◀ Silent But Deadly

Pirates hated to sink a valuable ship, so they preferred hand-to-hand fighting. Long knives were perfect for a surprise attack.

◀ **Meat-Loving Pirates**
The local Arawak people taught the settlers to cook meat over a smoky fire. The settlers became known as buccaneers, which means "barbecue men" in French.

THE BUCCANEERS

The buccaneers were French and English settlers who turned to piracy when Spanish forces forced them off their farms on the island of Hispaniola (now Haiti).

Calling themselves the "Brothers of the Coast," they roamed the Caribbean looking for ships to loot and soon developed a terrifying reputation.

Sextant

▲ **Port Royal**
The buccaneers were invited to drop anchor at Port Royal by Sir Thomas Modyford, the English governor of Jamaica. He hired them to attack ships belonging to his French, Dutch, and Spanish enemies.

Astrolabe ▶
Medieval sailors used this device to find their north-south position.

Tortuga Torturer

Buccaneer François L'Olonoise was one of the most vicious pirates. In one legend he cut out a prisoner's heart and began nibbling it while still asking his victim questions! He was eaten by cannibals after being shipwrecked in 1668.

Compass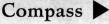

A compass needle always points north, showing which direction a ship is going.

Charts

To find a route across the sea, a pirate captain had to know where his ship was on the chart. Good charts showed the coastlines and hidden dangers such as reefs or rocks.

◀ Sextant

The captain measured his north-south position with a sextant. This measured the angle from the horizon to the sun when it was highest in the sky. The captain worked out how far east or west the ship was using a compass and by measuring the ship's speed.

Buccaneer Life ▶

The farmers who fled to Tortuga were joined by runaway slaves and escaped criminals. At first they survived by hunting wild cattle and turtles. Growing bolder, they began attacking Spanish ships. Daniel Montbars destroyed so many vessels he was nicknamed "The Exterminator!"

Musket

Rough linen shirt

Butcher's knives

Hunting dog

Leather breeches

Sir Henry Morgan

One of the luckiest pirates was Welshman Henry Morgan. He went to the Caribbean in 1655 as part of an English raid on the Spanish. By 1662, he had his own ship and captured several Spanish galleons.

In 1668, Morgan looted the rich city of Portobello in Cuba after marching through the jungle with 1,000 buccaneers. When he raided Panama in 1671, the Spanish complained to the English king, Charles II. Instead of punishing Morgan, Charles made him Sir Henry and governor of the island of Jamaica!

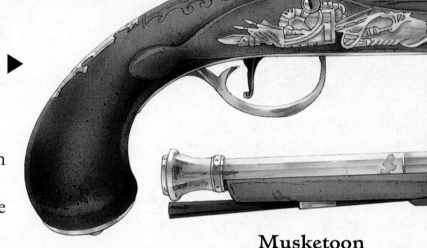

Pistols and Musketoons ▶
17th-century firearms fired a round lead ball. They were heavy and slow to load, but a single shot could easily kill an opponent. The longer barrel on a musketoon made it more accurate than a pistol.

Musketoon

Flint makes spark

Ball flies out of barrel

Gunpowder explodes

A Soggy Problem
A flintlock worked by creating a spark which set off the gunpowder inside the gun, forcing the ball out of the barrel. But damp powder at sea often caused flintlocks to misfire.

◀ Oliver Cromwell

The Pirate Hunter

The British force sent to capture Hispaniola by Oliver Cromwell ended up taking the island of Jamaica in 1655, which became an English base. When Henry Morgan was made governor, his main job was to hunt down pirates. Morgan was very good at this as he knew all their hiding places!

Pistol

▲ A Clever Trick

During a raid on the Spanish port of Maracaibo, Venezuela, in 1669, Morgan found his escape route blocked by three Spanish ships. As Morgan pretended to parlay with the Spanish, his men disguised a fire ship by fitting it with fake guns made from tree trunks and wooden sailors.

The trick worked and when one of the Spanish ships caught fire, Morgan made a quick getaway!

Surgeon's Tools ▶

Pirate crews expected casualties so did their best to make sure there was a surgeon on board, even if he was kidnapped! Wounds quickly went bad, so the surgeon had to work fast. The patient was given rum to lessen the pain while the damaged limb was sawn off.

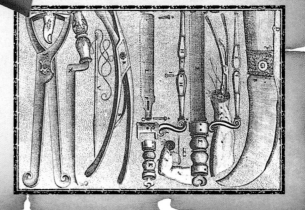

Cutlass
Blackbeard used a cutlass, a short slashing sword that was perfect for fighting on a crowded deck.

Smoky Terror
Blackbeard wove smoking fuses into his braids to make himself look even more scary!

BLACKBEARD

Edward Teach, known as "Blackbeard," became a legend in his own lifetime. After capturing a fine ship, *Queen Anne's Revenge*, in 1717, he raided Charleston in South Carolina and looted many ships in nearby waters.

For two years, Blackbeard spread terror along the east coast of America. He cut the fingers off prisoners who were too slow to hand over their rings, and forced others to eat their own ears after he had sliced them off.

Heads You Lose! ▶

Blackbeard's luck did not last. In 1718, British Navy officer Robert Maynard tricked Blackbeard into boarding his ship, by hiding his crew below deck. Blackbeard was wounded 25 times but only died when Maynard cut off his head!

Drunken Sailor

In the 1670s, Dutch buccaneer Roche Braziliano was famous for starting drunken brawls and shooting anyone who refused to have a ◀ drink with him.

Pirate Poet ▶

Ignoring the fact that most pirates were murdering thugs, the English writer Lord Byron made a pirate the hero of his poem, *The Corsair*, written in 1814.

PIRATE WOMEN

Anne Bonny fell in love with pirate Calico Jack Rackham, but the only way she could be with him was to dress like a man and join his crew!

In 1720, they were joined by another female pirate, Mary Read. The three rogues led many daring raids across the Caribbean. When the navy caught up with Jack, he gave himself up, but Anne and Mary fought like wildcats!

Anne Bonny

Pirate Tales ▶

Many pirate legends come from a famous book written by Charles Johnson in 1724 called *A General History of the Robberies and Murders of the Most Notorious Pirates.*

▼ "Calico" Jack

Rackham's nickname came from his brightly-colored cotton (calico) trousers.

Escaping the Hangman

After being captured, Rackham and his men were taken to Jamaica where they were hanged. As Mary and Anne were pregnant, they could not be executed. Mary died in prison but Anne lived to be 81!

Grace O'Malley ▶
This 16th-century pirate ruled the seas off the west coast of Ireland. In one story, she kidnapped the grandson of an Earl when he refused to invite her for dinner. Her ransom was that he and his family would forever lay an extra place at dinner for her.

Mary
Read

▲ **Women Pirates**
Some pirates had wives but they left them ashore as women were banned on board ship. However, there had always been women pirates. In one legend, the Viking Princess Alwilda led her own pirate ship in the 9th century. Around 250 BC, Queen Teuta's pirate fleet terrorized the Adriatic Sea until she was defeated by a fleet of 200 Roman ships.

PIRATE LIFE

Life at sea was tough—pirates had to climb the rigging, raise the anchor, clean rusty weapons, mend torn sails, and stop any leaks. In battle, the crew fired the cannons as well as taking part in hand-to-hand fighting.

Back on shore after a raid, pirates liked nothing better than a sing-along and a dance after a hearty meal. Others spent their booty on drink, women, and gambling.

▼ Divers have recovered many everyday items from the pirate haunt Port Royal (now underwater).

Glass bottle

Pewter mug

Clay pipe

Food and Drink

Though pigs and chickens were brought on board as food, these were soon eaten. A typical pirate meal was salted meat or dried fish, a tot of rum or wine, and ship's crackers.

Turtles were also caught at sea and kept alive in a tank of water until they were eaten. Eating limes helped protect pirates from a disease called scurvy, caused by a lack of vitamin C.

Limes

▲ Careening and Keelhauling

At sea, a ship's hull was soon covered in crusty barnacles that slowed it down. Pirates sailed the ship inshore then let the vessel tip over as the tide went out. The barnacles were then scraped off, known as careening. The rough sides were also used to torture rebellious crew members who were dragged under the boat by a rope tied to their hands and feet, known as keelhauling. ▶

◀ A Captain's Share

A captain got the biggest share of any loot. As a result, there were often fights to become captain!

◀ Long John Silver

Most people's idea of a pirate is Long John Silver, a peg-legged rogue with a parrot on his shoulder. He's not a real pirate but a character from Robert Louis Stevenson's book *Treasure Island*, written in 1883.

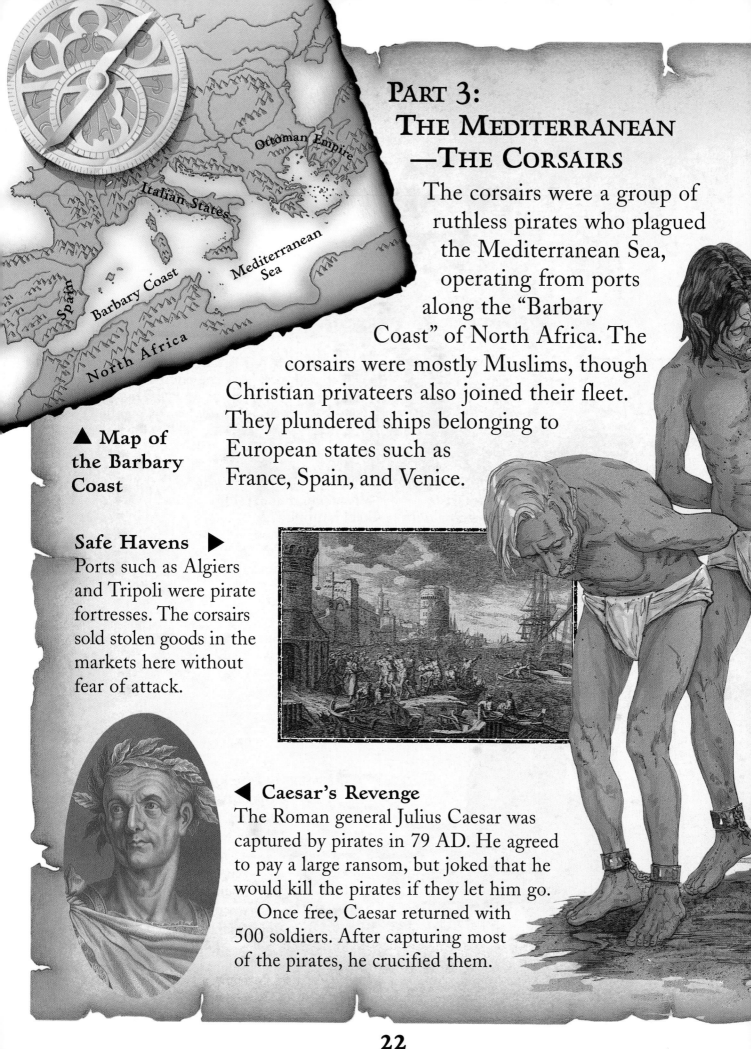

PART 3: THE MEDITERRANEAN —THE CORSAIRS

The corsairs were a group of ruthless pirates who plagued the Mediterranean Sea, operating from ports along the "Barbary Coast" of North Africa. The corsairs were mostly Muslims, though Christian privateers also joined their fleet. They plundered ships belonging to European states such as France, Spain, and Venice.

▲ **Map of the Barbary Coast**

Safe Havens ▶
Ports such as Algiers and Tripoli were pirate fortresses. The corsairs sold stolen goods in the markets here without fear of attack.

◀ **Caesar's Revenge**
The Roman general Julius Caesar was captured by pirates in 79 AD. He agreed to pay a large ransom, but joked that he would kill the pirates if they let him go.
Once free, Caesar returned with 500 soldiers. After capturing most of the pirates, he crucified them.

22

Freed! ▶
In 1815, when the British Navy attacked Algiers, 3,000 prisoners were freed from the corsairs.

◀ **Slave Traders**
The corsairs took prisoners as well as loot. Anyone who wasn't rich enough to pay a ransom was sold as a slave. They were taken to a huge prison known as the "bagnio" where they stayed at night. During the day they worked as servants or as galley slaves.

THE BROTHERS BARBAROSSA

The most feared corsairs were two brothers called Barbarossa, or "red beard." The elder brother, Aruj, began life as a pirate by seizing two galleys belonging to the Pope. By 1516, his fleet was strong enough to capture the port of Algiers.

The King of Spain sent 10,000 men to attack Aruj. When he died in 1518, his younger brother, Kheir-ed-Din, took control. Helped by the Turks, he began a reign of terror that lasted 30 years!

▲ Turkish Support
The Turkish Sultan Selim I, based in Istanbul, gave Kheir-ed-Din 2,000 troops to protect him against the Spanish forces. In return, Kheir-ed-Din's fleet became part of the Sultan's navy.

Brothers Barbarossa

▲ Swallows and Amazons
The children in Arthur Ransome's book *Swallows and Amazons* get their ideas from pirates. Their boat flies the Jolly Roger and they call their uncle Captain Flint (a famous pirate).

Jolly Roger ▶
The pirate flag was called the Jolly Roger, from the French *jolie rouge* meaning "pretty red," as the first pirate flags were red.

Later flags were black, and many pirates made up their own design.

◀ **Muslim Marauders**
The Corsairs wore the flowing robes common in North Africa. Most were Muslims, but Christians such as Simon Danziger were allowed to join the corsairs as they knew how to sail in the stormy waters of the Atlantic ocean.

Christopher Condent

Calico Jack Rackham

Edward England

Thomas Tew

Blackbeard

Emmanuel Wynne

THE CORSAIR GALLEY

The corsairs fought in fast galleys rowed by slaves as they could not rely on good winds in the calm waters of the Mediterranean.

Hunting in packs, they attacked by boarding or ramming their target. Some corsairs disguised their galleys as merchant ships to trick their victims. Others terrified the crew into giving up without a fight.

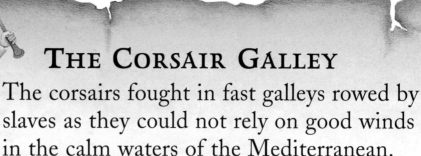

▲ Dragut Reis

Dragut Reis was one of the most feared corsairs. As well as looting ships, he raided the Italian coast and conquered most of Tunisia from the Spanish. When he captured the island of Gozo, he sold the entire population, around 6,000 people, as slaves.

The Ram ▼

Ramming a ship punched a hole in the hull, while making a bridge for the boarding party.

◄ Built for Speed

The long slender shape of the corsair galleys made them very fast.

Easy Pickings ▶

Early cargo ships were slow and rarely sailed far from the coast, making them an easy target for pirates lurking in ambush.

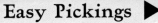

◀ Ancient Pirates

As their Empire grew, the Romans wiped out most of the pirates in the Mediterranean. However, Greek pirates used the Lipari Islands north of Sicily as a base for over 2,500 years.

▼ Into Battle

Most battles were decided by hand-to-hand fighting. The corsairs' favorite weapons were muskets, knives, and curved swords known as scimitars.

▲ Galley Slaves

It took around 200 men to row a corsair galley. The conditions were terrible. The slaves were chained to the ship and whipped to make them row! Once a day they were given a cracker, oil, and vinegar.

PIRATE ATTACK!

As most pirate ships were smaller than the galleons they attacked, they relied on hit and run attacks. A common ploy was to hoist a friendly flag. Meanwhile, the boarding party hid below deck, armed to the teeth. At the last minute, the pirates hoisted the Jolly Roger and opened fire. They leapt onto the enemy ship before the crew could defend themselves.

Night Raid ▶

Some pirates attacked at night using small boats or canoes. They would sneak up behind the ship, where there were no cannons to shoot back at them. Then they shot the crew on deck with their muskets. Finally, they climbed on board using iron hooks tied to a long rope.

Walking the plank

▲ No mercy!

Any of the merchant crew who fought back would be killed and their bodies fed to the sharks. Were captives forced to walk the plank? Probably not, as pirates wouldn't want to waste any time. But pirates did set fire to their victims or shot them from cannons.

Sneaky Tricks ▶

An easy way to capture a ship was to get invited on board. In one story, the pirates dressed up as women, so the crew of the merchant ship thought they were safe from attack!

Another trick was to tow ropes behind the pirate ship to slow it down, so it looked like a merchant ship with a heavy cargo.

◀ **Long Drop**

Pirates who were caught faced the death penalty. In Britain they were hanged. Huge crowds came to watch the executions.

On Show ▶

After the execution, the last words of pirates were often printed in pamphlets. Some pirates had their head stuck on a pole as a warning to others.

PART 4: THE INDIAN OCEAN—SILKS AND SPICES

Arab and Indian pirates raided shipping for hundreds of years before Portuguese captain Vasco da Gama became the first European to reach India by sea in 1498. Merchant ships flocked to India from Portugal, Britain, and Holland, closely followed by pirates from all over the globe. The Indian Ocean was soon crawling with rogues such as Thomas Tew, Henry Avery, and William Kidd.

▲ **Lovely Loot**
Silks, spices, and jewels carried across the Indian Ocean attracted pirates from the Caribbean.

▲ **The Gujarati Rovers**
From the 1300s, the Gujarati Rovers cruised the Indian Ocean in fleets of 20 to 30 ships. They made prisoners who swallowed jewelry throw up by forcing them to swallow the bitter tamarind root.

▼ The Dhow
Indian and Arab pirates sailed in dhows, sailing ships with a slender shape and a triangular sail.

◄ Pirate Fashion
While some pirates wore bright clothing and jewelry, most were happy with a strong leather belt and a decent pair of boots. A silk scarf tied around the waist could be used to hold a pair of pistols.

▲ Pet or Prize?
Pirates in South America did capture parrots, not for themselves, but for sale as exotic pets back in Europe.

▲ Branded!
By the 1700s, the British East India Company was policing the Indian Ocean. Any pirates who escaped hanging were whipped and branded—a red hot iron burned a "P" on their forehead.

THE PIRATE KINGDOM

The island of Madagascar in the Indian Ocean was a popular haunt for buccaneers from the Caribbean. They set up bases along the coast, known as "kingdoms." St. Mary's Island, the largest kingdom, was home to 17 ships and 1,500 pirates. However, the buccaneers used most of the jewels and silks they robbed to buy supplies. Within 30 years only a few poor, lonely pirates remained.

Pirate Fantasy ▶

Back in Europe, people told fantastic stories of pirate kings living in luxury. In fact, most pirates wasted their money drinking and gambling.

▼ Robinson Crusoe

Daniel Defoe's story *Robinson Crusoe* was based on the adventures of Scottish sailor Alexander Selkirk. Selkirk spent four years stuck on a desert island after being marooned there by his captain, William Dampier.

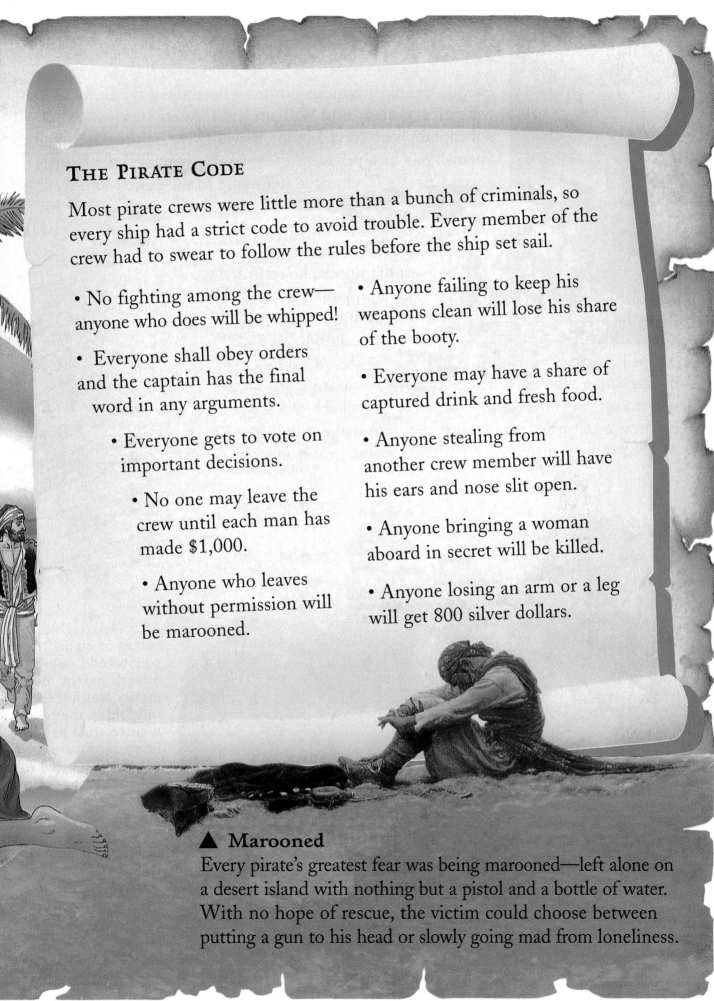

THE PIRATE CODE

Most pirate crews were little more than a bunch of criminals, so every ship had a strict code to avoid trouble. Every member of the crew had to swear to follow the rules before the ship set sail.

- No fighting among the crew—anyone who does will be whipped!

- Everyone shall obey orders and the captain has the final word in any arguments.

- Everyone gets to vote on important decisions.

- No one may leave the crew until each man has made $1,000.

- Anyone who leaves without permission will be marooned.

- Anyone failing to keep his weapons clean will lose his share of the booty.

- Everyone may have a share of captured drink and fresh food.

- Anyone stealing from another crew member will have his ears and nose slit open.

- Anyone bringing a woman aboard in secret will be killed.

- Anyone losing an arm or a leg will get 800 silver dollars.

▲ Marooned

Every pirate's greatest fear was being marooned—left alone on a desert island with nothing but a pistol and a bottle of water. With no hope of rescue, the victim could choose between putting a gun to his head or slowly going mad from loneliness.

AVERY AND KIDD

On his first voyage, Henry Avery captured the biggest prize in pirate history. Sailing to the Indian Ocean, Avery chased the treasure ship *Ganj-i-Sawai* for eight days before capturing it in a ferocious battle. This raid earned Avery over £350,000. Soon afterward, he returned to England, then vanished!

In 1695, a group of New York businessmen paid William Kidd to catch pirates in the Indian Ocean. After killing one of his crew with a bucket, he turned to piracy. When he captured the *Quedah Merchant*, he hid most of the stolen treasure on an island.

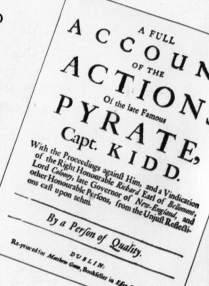

A FULL
ACCOUNT
OF THE
ACTIONS
Of the late Famous
PYRATE,
Capt. KIDD.
With the Proceedings against Him, and a Vindication of the Right Honourable *Richard* Earl of *Bellomont*, Lord *Colony*, late Governor of *New-England*, and other Honourable Persons, from the Unjust Reflections cast upon tehm.

By a Person of Quality.

DUBLIN:
Re-printed for *Matthew Gunn*, Bookseller in *Essex-Street*, 1701.

◀ **Who's Dinner?**
Pirates restocked their food supplies by stealing from other ships' stores.

When pirate Charlotte de Berry's crew ran out of food, they drew lots to see who would be eaten by the others. De Berry's husband was the unlucky loser!

Peter Pan

▼ Captain Hook

The famous storybook pirate Captain Hook appears in the novel *Peter Pan*, written by J. M. Barrie. Hook has an iron hook instead of a right hand, which was cut off by Peter Pan and eaten by a crocodile.

His character may be based on Welsh pirate Bartholemew Roberts, who dressed in a crimson vest and wore a red feather in his hat.

Captain Kidd

◄ Hanged!

When Kidd arrived back in New York, hoping for a pardon, his business partners deserted him. Kidd was arrested and sent to London to be hanged as a pirate. A drunken Kidd wriggled about so much that the rope snapped. The hangman tried again. This time it worked. Kidd's dead body was then covered in tar and left to hang for several years as a warning to other pirates.

THE MARATHAS

The most successful pirate in the Indian Ocean was Kanhoji Angria. In the 1690s, he led the Maratha pirates living along the Malabar coast of west India. Sailing in fast ships known as "grabs," they plundered ships belonging to the British East India Company.

For almost 25 years the British could do little to stop Angria. His fleet was too large and giant forts defended his pirate bases.

▼ Booty!

After a raid, the pirates shared out the booty. The captain and quartermaster (officer in charge of stores) each got two shares. The master gunner and boatswain got one and a half shares, while the rest of the crew got one share.

▲ Sir William James

In 1751, James was made commander of the East India Company's navy. Within five years he had destroyed the Angrian pirate fleet.

▲ Pieces of Eight
To most pirates treasure usually meant gold and silver. The Spanish often turned gold and silver objects into coins before bringing them back to Europe.

The famous pieces of eight were silver coins worth eight Spanish *reales*.

▲ Last Stand at Severndroog
During 1755, Sir William James destroyed the Maratha pirate bases one by one until only the Angrian fort at Severndroog survived. In a bold attack, James sailed his ship the *Protector* close to the fort and opened fire. The fort blew up when one shot hit the gunpowder storeroom.

A Pirate Ship

When pirates came across a ship they liked, they stole it! Most preferred a fast ship that was easy to handle and had a shallow keel. This allowed them to hide in bays and rivers not deep enough for warships.

Most pirates liked to attack fast and disappear quickly rather than get caught up in a long gun battle. Their ships had fewer cannons than warships as a heavy cannon slowed a vessel down.

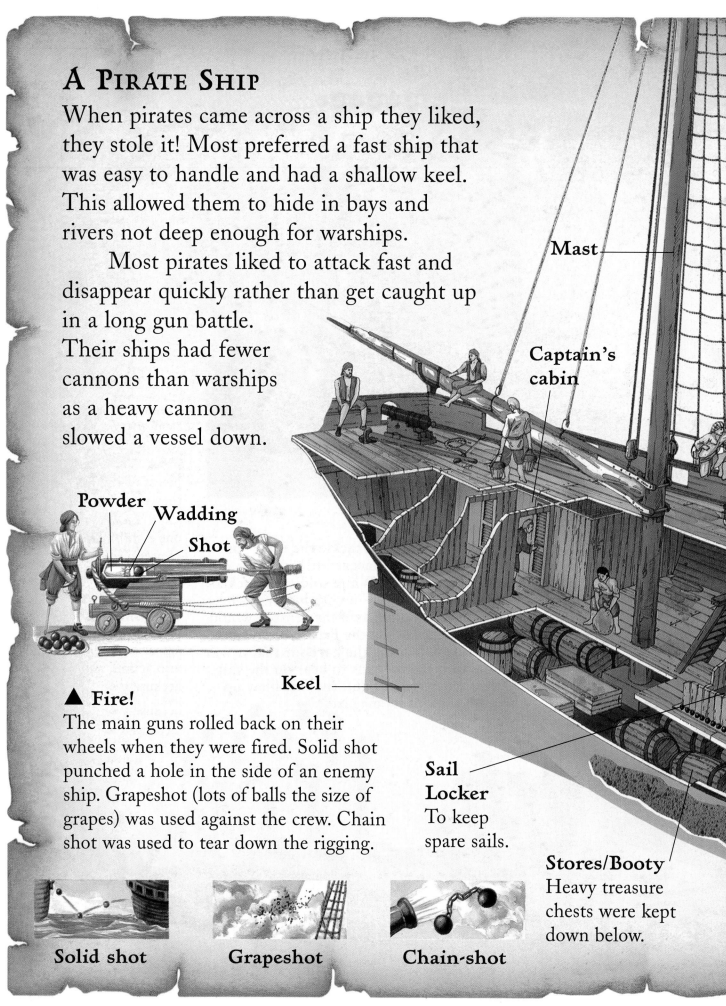

Mast

Captain's cabin

Powder

Wadding

Shot

Keel

Sail Locker
To keep spare sails.

Stores/Booty
Heavy treasure chests were kept down below.

▲ **Fire!**
The main guns rolled back on their wheels when they were fired. Solid shot punched a hole in the side of an enemy ship. Grapeshot (lots of balls the size of grapes) was used against the crew. Chain shot was used to tear down the rigging.

Solid shot

Grapeshot

Chain-shot

Hoist the Main Sail!

Small vessels such as sloops and schooners were fast because they carried a lot of sails for their size.

To turn them into fighting ships, pirates tore away the upper decks to create a clear fighting space. Holes were cut in the sides to make gun ports.

▼ Below Decks

Pirates lived in dark, damp quarters smelling of dirty bilge water, the tar used to stop leaks in the hull, and unwashed bodies!

The pirates slept in hammocks, which were originally invented by the local peoples of the Caribbean.

Rigging
The ropes that held the mast and sails in place.

Galley
The ship's kitchen.

Windlass
A winding machine hauled up the heavy sails.

Anchor
A heavy iron anchor kept the ship moored to the seabed.

Ballast
Heavy rocks kept the ship upright.

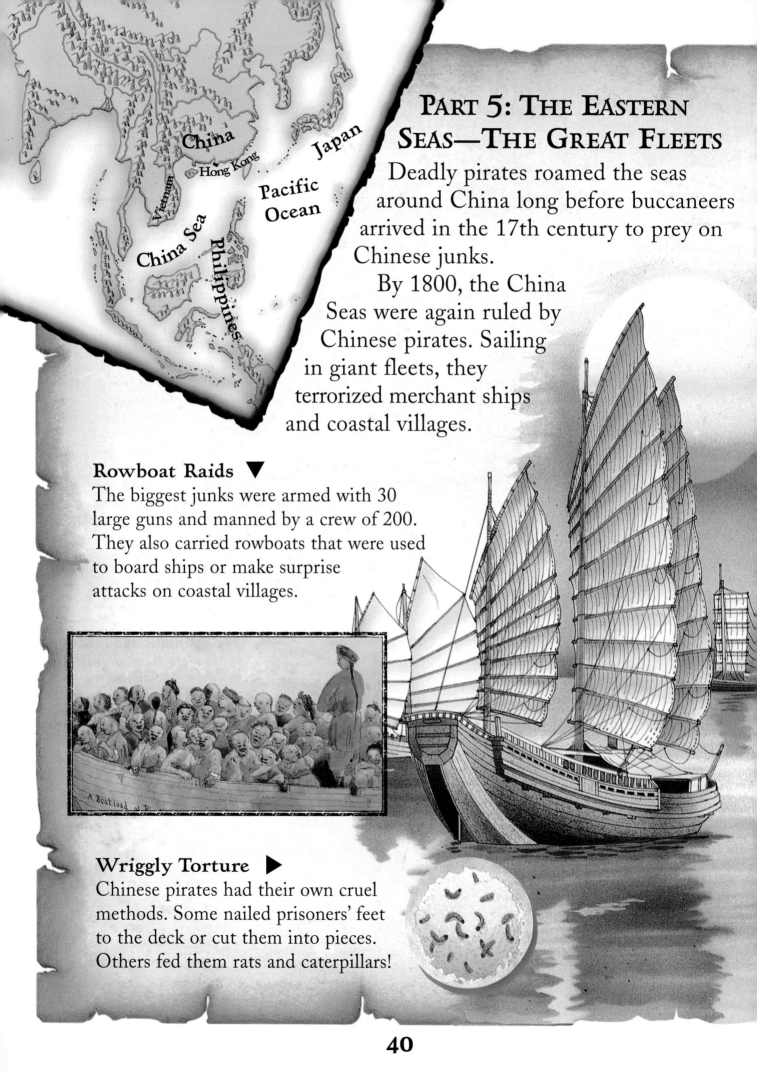

PART 5: THE EASTERN SEAS—THE GREAT FLEETS

Deadly pirates roamed the seas around China long before buccaneers arrived in the 17th century to prey on Chinese junks.

By 1800, the China Seas were again ruled by Chinese pirates. Sailing in giant fleets, they terrorized merchant ships and coastal villages.

Rowboat Raids ▼

The biggest junks were armed with 30 large guns and manned by a crew of 200. They also carried rowboats that were used to board ships or make surprise attacks on coastal villages.

A Boatload of P...

Wriggly Torture ▶

Chinese pirates had their own cruel methods. Some nailed prisoners' feet to the deck or cut them into pieces. Others fed them rats and caterpillars!

A Floating Home ▶

Pirates converted cargo junks by adding guns. Each junk was a family home as well as a fighting ship. The captain's wife and children lived with him in a cabin while the crew's families lived in the ship's hold or on deck.

Chinese Pirate Fleet

Weapons

Eastern pirates made good use of European weapons such as muskets and swiveling cannons. In hand-to-hand fighting, they used traditional weapons such as swords, spears, axes, and blowpipes.

▼ Dao sword

Pirates in Borneo used this sword in the 1870s. It is decorated with human hair.

◀ The Silky Pirate

Chinese pirate Cheng Chih-Lung led a fleet of 1,000 junks and a private army of Dutch and African warriors for over 20 years. Famous for wearing brightly-colored silk clothing, he controlled the South China Seas from Japan to Vietnam.

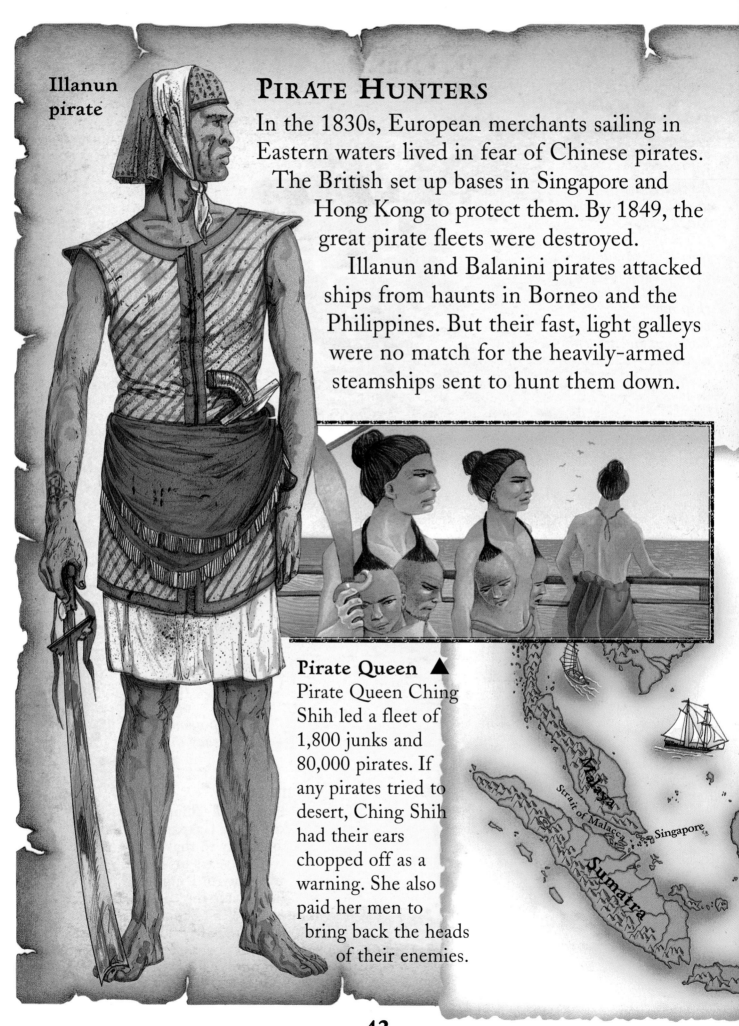

Illanun pirate

PIRATE HUNTERS

In the 1830s, European merchants sailing in Eastern waters lived in fear of Chinese pirates. The British set up bases in Singapore and Hong Kong to protect them. By 1849, the great pirate fleets were destroyed.

Illanun and Balanini pirates attacked ships from haunts in Borneo and the Philippines. But their fast, light galleys were no match for the heavily-armed steamships sent to hunt them down.

Pirate Queen ▲
Pirate Queen Ching Shih led a fleet of 1,800 junks and 80,000 pirates. If any pirates tried to desert, Ching Shih had their ears chopped off as a warning. She also paid her men to bring back the heads of their enemies.

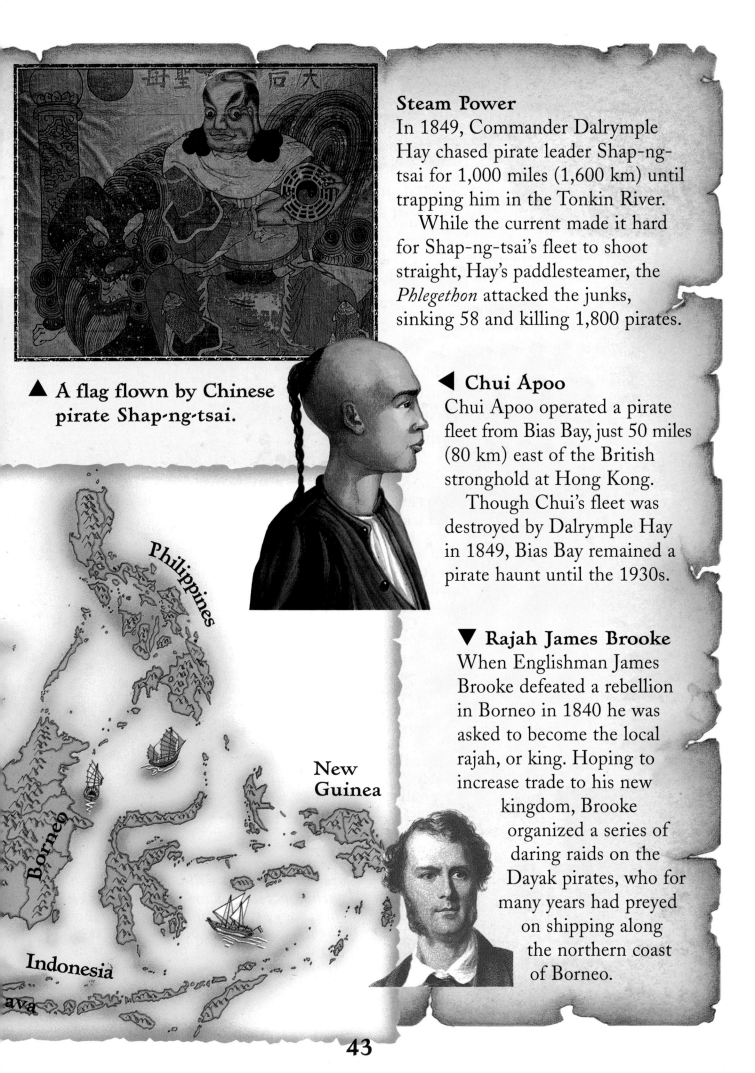

Steam Power

In 1849, Commander Dalrymple Hay chased pirate leader Shap-ng-tsai for 1,000 miles (1,600 km) until trapping him in the Tonkin River.

While the current made it hard for Shap-ng-tsai's fleet to shoot straight, Hay's paddlesteamer, the *Phlegethon* attacked the junks, sinking 58 and killing 1,800 pirates.

▲ A flag flown by Chinese pirate Shap-ng-tsai.

◀ **Chui Apoo**

Chui Apoo operated a pirate fleet from Bias Bay, just 50 miles (80 km) east of the British stronghold at Hong Kong.

Though Chui's fleet was destroyed by Dalrymple Hay in 1849, Bias Bay remained a pirate haunt until the 1930s.

▼ **Rajah James Brooke**

When Englishman James Brooke defeated a rebellion in Borneo in 1840 he was asked to become the local rajah, or king. Hoping to increase trade to his new kingdom, Brooke organized a series of daring raids on the Dayak pirates, who for many years had preyed on shipping along the northern coast of Borneo.

Philippines

New Guinea

Borneo

Indonesia

ava

TODAY'S PIRATES

Piracy is still very much alive. In 2008, there were 293 attacks on ships, with a higher total expected for 2009. Today's pirates attack from speedboats using modern satellite tracking, machine guns, and rockets to hunt their victims. Many prey on cargo ships as they slow down sailing through narrow straits.

A common tactic is for one boat to attack from the front. While the ship tries to avoid a crash, two other boats sneak up from behind and board it.

▼ Queen of the Macao Pirates

In the 1920s, Lai Choi San, or the "Dragon Lady," led a pirate fleet in the waters around Macao. Known for her cunning and cruelty, she made a great fortune by raiding ships and ransoming prisoners.

Lai vanished mysteriously in the 1930s. In one legend her ship was hit by a Japanese torpedo; in another she was put in jail but later she escaped.

Merchant Targets

In Nigeria and Southeast Asia, pirates attack ships carrying oil. Some sail a captured ship to a nearby port where they repaint it and give it a new identity.

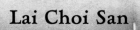

Lai Choi San

Hijack Tactics

In 2008, Somalian pirates took the crew of a French luxury yacht hostage. After the ransom was paid and the hostages released, French commandoes carried out a daring helicopter raid and seized six pirates.

▲ Luxury Targets

The waters off the coast of Somalia are now swarming with pirates. Pirates are also returning to the Caribbean in big numbers. In both regions the targets are not cargo ships but luxury yachts. No one navy patrols international waters. In 2003, Taskforce 150 was set up to help navies from around the world work together in the fight against piracy.

▼ A patrol investigates a suspicious fishing boat.

Refugee Attacks

In the 1980s, Thai pirates robbed, kidnapped, or killed tens of thousands of helpless refugees leaving Vietnam.

PIRATE WORDS

Bagnio—A prison use by Muslim corsairs to hold Christian prisoners.

Ballast— The heavy weight at the bottom of a sailing vessel used to keep it upright.

Barbary Coast—Northwest coast of Africa.

Bilge—The area at the bottom of a ship where water collects.

Buccaneer—A Caribbean pirate.

Careening—Scraping marine life from the bottom of a boat.

Chart—A sailor's map (see below).

Corsair—A Mediterranean pirate.

Dhow—An Arab sailing vessel with a single triangular sail.

Galleon—A large sailing ship with three masts.

Hammock—A rope or canvas sling used as a bed.

Hispaniola—The original Spanish name for the island which now comprises Haiti and the Dominican Republic.

Jolly Roger—The pirate flag, showing a skull and crossbones.

Junk—A Chinese sailing vessel.

Maroon—Abandon, usually on a deserted island or coastline.

Navigate—To find your way at sea.

New World—The Americas (above).

Outlaw—A criminal living beyond the protection of the law.

Pieces of Eight—Gold coins worth a dollar.

Privateer—A sea raider operating with his government's permission.

Prize—A captured ship.

Rais—A sea captain in the Muslim world.

Rigging—The ropes supporting masts and sails.

Scurvy—A disease caused by lack of vitamin C.

Stem (or stern)—The back of a ship.

Trireme—A galley built by the Ancient Greeks with oarsmen on three levels (see diagram, right).

PIRATE TIMELINE

3000 BC Egyptians first use ships for long voyages. Beginning of piracy.

1200-600 BC Greek raiders rule eastern Mediterranean.

400 AD Chinese pirate San Wen ravages northern coast of China.

800-1000 AD Vikings raid towns and attack ships, from Iceland to the Black Sea.

1290 Marco Polo warns of Gujarati pirates in the Indian Ocean.

1492 Columbus' first voyage to America.

1496-1540 Spanish conquest of New World. Rise of piracy in the Caribbean.

1497 Vasco da Gama opens sea route to India and China.

1560 Dragut Reis defeats Spanish.

1562-1585 English privateers attack the Spanish Main.

1627-1646 Ching Chih-lung terrorizes Chinese coast.

1630-1654 Spanish troops clear buccaneers from Hispaniola.

1655-1680 British governors of Jamaica urge buccaneers to make Port Royal their base.

1670s Buccaneers at their peak in the Caribbean and Indian Ocean.

1690-1720 Madagascar becomes main base of European pirates in Indian Ocean.

1690-1729 Kanhoji Angria builds up fleet. Maratha Wars begin.

1692 Port Royal is flattened by a massive earthquake. 2,000 people die.

1718 Captain Maynard hunts Blackbeard down and kills him.

1720 Mary Read, Anne Bonny, and Calico Jack are captured.

1755 William James destroys Severndroog, ending the Maratha Wars.

1800s Ching Yih and Ching Shih control fleet of 1,800 junks and 80,000 pirates.

1830 French invade Algiers, ending the threat from corsairs.

1841 Founding of Hong Kong ends great Chinese pirate fleets.

2000s A new wave of piracy in Africa, Indonesia, and Caribbean.

INDEX

Alwilda, Princess 19
Angria, Kanhoji 36
Avery, Henry 30, 34

Barbarossa brothers 24
Barbary Coast 7, 22, 23
Blackbeard (Edward Teach) 16-17
Bonny, Anne 18-19
Brooke, Rajah James 43
buccaneers 12, 13, 14, 30, 32, 46
Byron, Lord 17

Caesar, Julius 22
Caribbean 6, 10-11, 12, 16, 18, 45
Chinese piracy 40-41, 42-43, 44
Cheng Chih-Lung 41
Ching Shih 42
Chui Apoo 43
Columbus, Christopher 10
Conquistadors 11
corsairs 7, 17, 22, 23

Dampier, William 11, 32
Danziger, Simon 25
De Berry, Charlotte 34
Dragut Reis 26
Drake, Sir Francis 7

eastern seas 7, 40-45

female pirates 18-19, 44
fictional pirates 6, 9, 12, 17, 21, 24, 35

galleons 10, 46
Gujarati Rovers 30

Hanseatic League 8
Hispaniola 12, 13, 15
Hook, Captain 6, 35

Indian Ocean 7, 30-39

Jamaica 12, 14, 15
James, Sir William 36-37
Jolly Roger 25, 46

keel-hauling 21
Kidd, William 19, 30, 34, 35

Lai Choi San 44
L'Olonoise, François 13

Madagascar 7, 32
Maratha Wars 36-37
Mediterranean 7, 22-29
modern piracy 44-45
Montbars, Daniel 13
Morgan, Sir Henry 14-15

navigation 13, 46
northern Europe 7, 8-9

O'Malley, Grace 19

pieces of eight 37, 46
pirate ships 8, 9, 10-11, 26-27, 31, 38-39, 40-41
Plantain, James 19, 32
Port Royal, Jamaica 12
privateers 7, 22, 46
punishment for piracy 31, 35

Rackham, "Calico Jack" 18
Read, Mary 18-19

Shap-ng-tsai 43
sickness and disease 15, 20
Silver, Long John 6, 21
slaves 22, 23, 27
Spanish Main 10-21
St. Patrick 9

Teuta, Queen 19
Tew, Thomas 30

Vikings 8, 9, 19

weapons 11, 14, 16, 41

Photocredits. Unless otherwise stated all pictures in this book were supplied by the National Maritime Museum, London, and we gratefully acknowledge their assistance. The publishers are also grateful to the following for their permission to reproduce pictures and photographs: (*Abbreviations: t—top, m—middle, b—bottom, r—right, l—left*) 4-5, 7, 12m, 17b, 18 both, 19, 32, 34m: Hulton Deutsch Collection; 6m: United Artists (Courtesy Kobal); 6b: Warner Bros (Courtesy Kobal); 8, 11t, 13, 1St, 17t, 21, 27t, 35 both, 43b: Mary Evans Picture Library; 11m, 47t: Solution Pictures; 12b: © John Ryan (from the book Captain Pugwash, a Pirate Story); 22b: Poseidon Pictures; 24t, 45m & b: Frank Spooner Pictures; 24b: Theatre Projects Films (Courtesy Kobal); 33, 36-37: Delaware Art Museum, Howard Pyle Collection; 45 Spectrum Colour Library.